JOEY
the supersocks hero

This book belongs to

....

....

Vision Street Publishing Llc.
2900 Glades Circle, Suite 850
Weston, Florida, C.P. 33327
USA
www.visionstreetpub.com
Tel.: +1(954) 626 3789

Author and Editor:
Dilpreet Kaur and Rennie Thomas

This edition is published in 2019
Printed in India, March 2019
First edition.

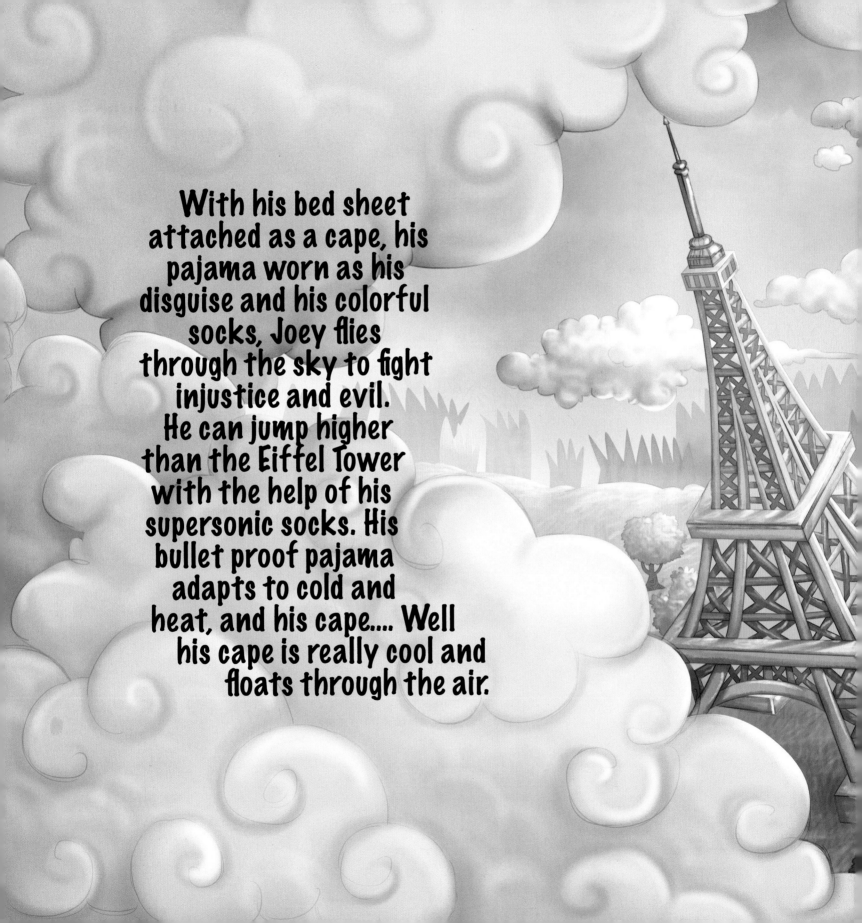

With his bed sheet attached as a cape, his pajama worn as his disguise and his colorful socks, Joey flies through the sky to fight injustice and evil. He can jump higher than the Eiffel Tower with the help of his supersonic socks. His bullet proof pajama adapts to cold and heat, and his cape.... Well his cape is really cool and floats through the air.

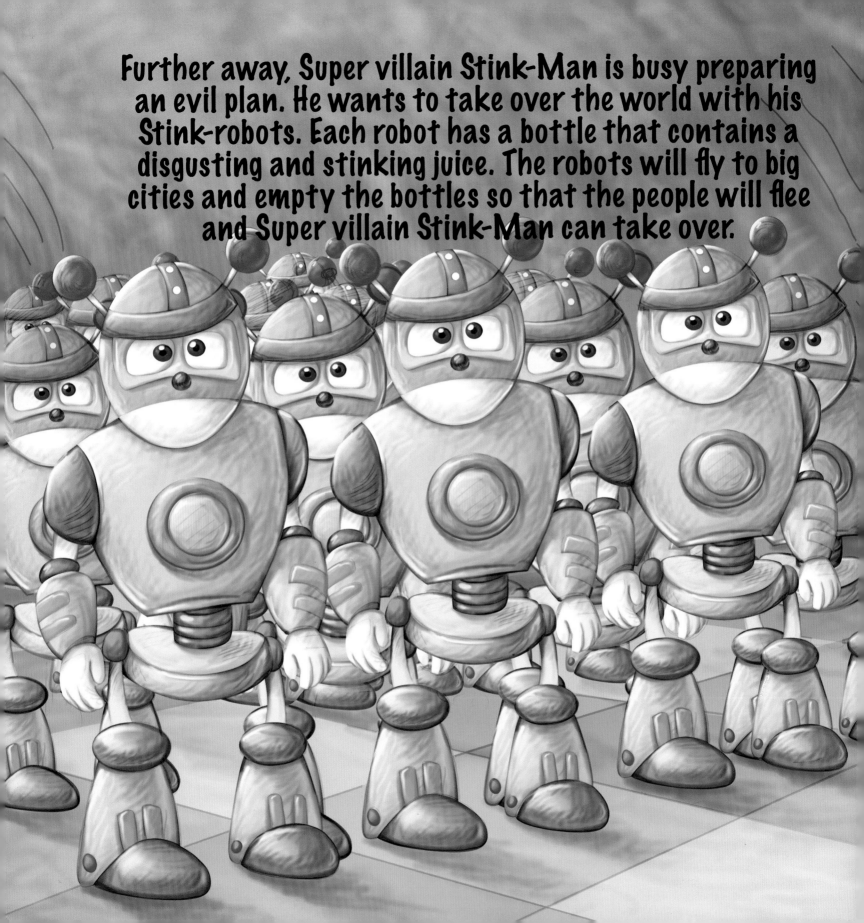

Further away, Super villain Stink-Man is busy preparing an evil plan. He wants to take over the world with his Stink-robots. Each robot has a bottle that contains a disgusting and stinking juice. The robots will fly to big cities and empty the bottles so that the people will flee and Super villain Stink-Man can take over.

Joey is at school and has his supersonic socks on. The rest of his costume is hidden in his backpack in the corridor. The lesson is really boring and Joey has trouble not falling asleep.

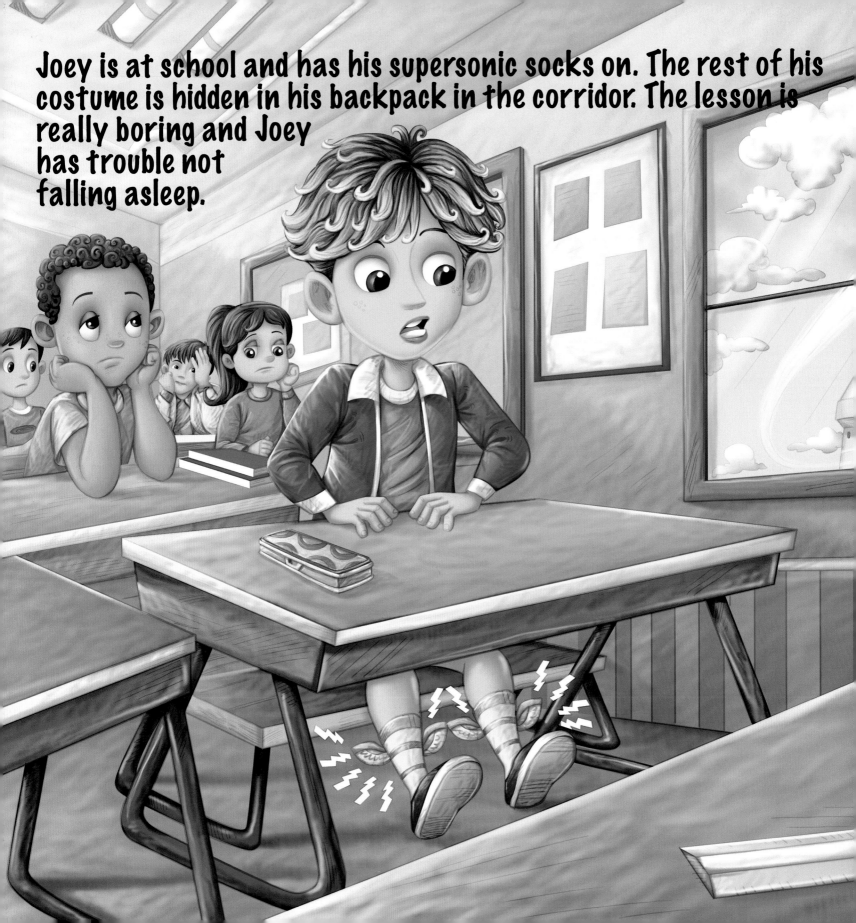

Suddenly he sees through the window a stink-robot flying by really fast. Joey's socks are starting to tingle. This means the world needs Joey the Supersocks hero!

Joey runs out to the corridor and grabs his backpack. On his way to the toilet, he already starts to change, almost falling on his way. His pajama and cape are on. He's ready!

Joey already knew that this can only be the work of Supervillain Stink-Man.

Supervillain Stink-Man is sitting behind his big screen and is watching all his stink-robots flying out. "I am such an evil Supervillain! My plan is brilliant!"

A deep and mean laugh echoes through the walls of the cave
where Supervillain Stink-Man is hiding. He almost jumps at his
own sound, "MWAAHAAHAAHAAHAAHAA!"

Joey is now a real super hero. He makes big jumps in the sky. But where is he going? Where would Super villain Stink-man hide?

Joey is thinking the most logical answer would be somewhere nobody could be bothered with his smell. Where can that be?

The ice cold South pole of course!

"Here I come, mean smelly villain!" screams Joey while flying through the sky.

But before Joey goes on, he makes a stop at the super market around the corner to buy a clothes pin. There is a long row of people waiting to pay. Once it's Joey's turn, the cashier calls, "One clothes pin for this young man!"

Joey leaves the shop and places the clothespin on his nose. That was a smart move!

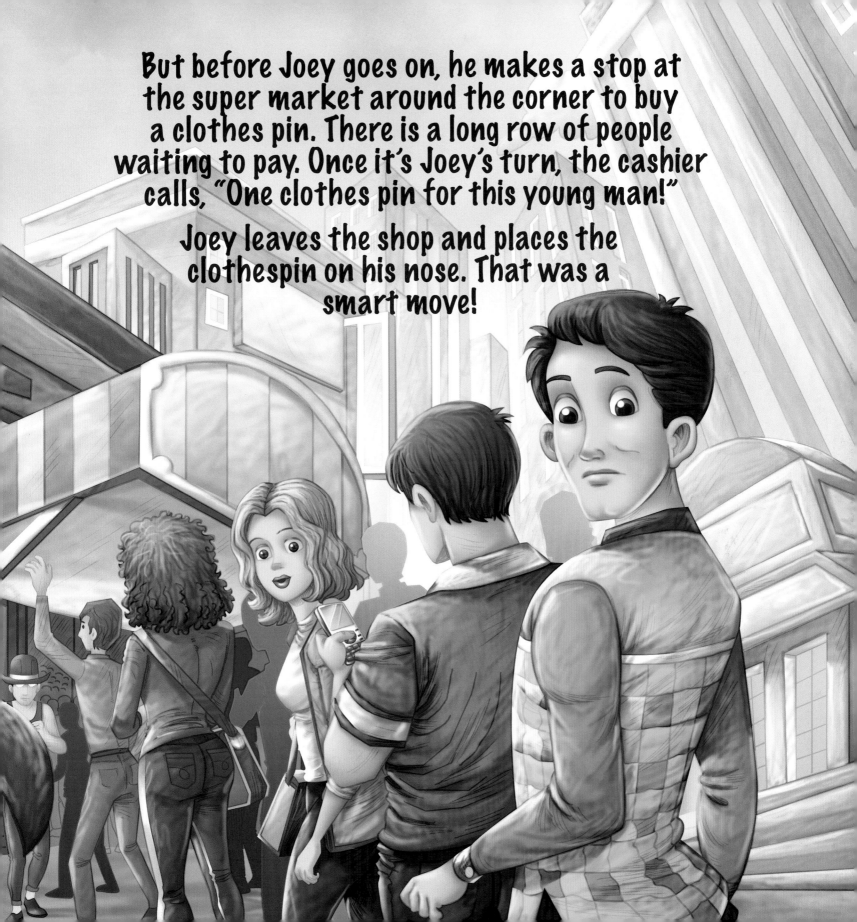

The Stink-robots are approaching their respective destination. In a lot of big cities, the robots have already landed. There is one on the Statue of Liberty in NY, one on the Pisa tower in Italy, one on the Eiffel tower in Paris and another one on Big Ben in London. Further away, you can already see that one robot landed on the Chinese Wall and one on the Opera building in Sydney.

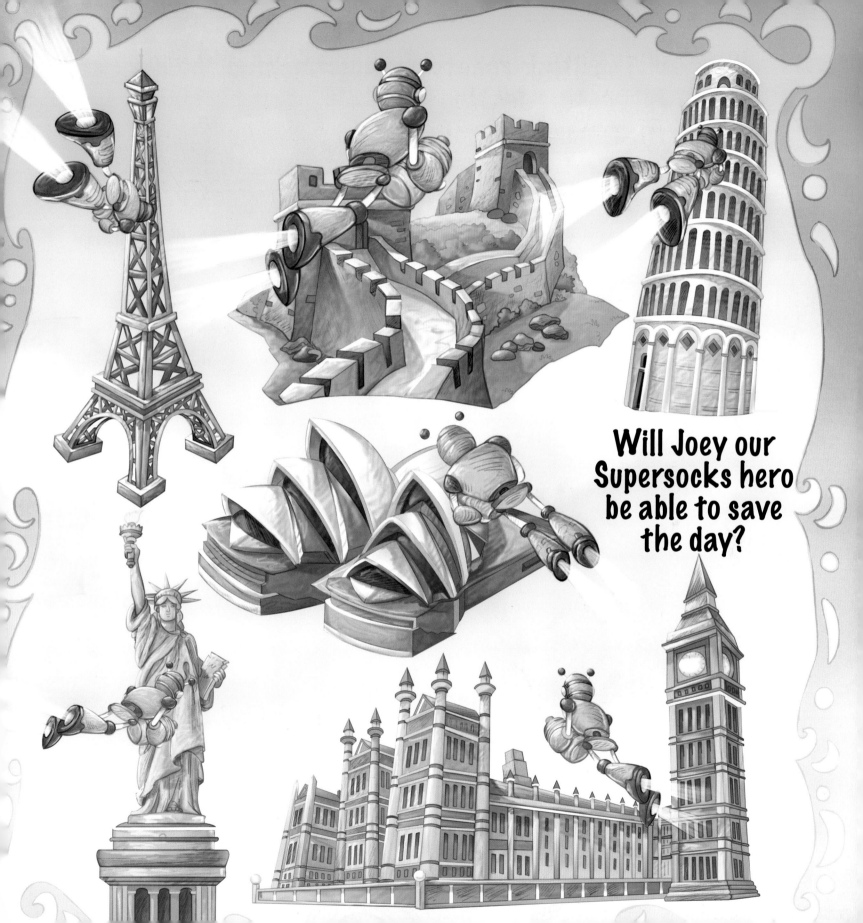

Will Joey our Supersocks hero be able to save the day?

Joey's supersonic socks are tingling more and more as he approaches the Southpole. He knows it's a sign he is getting closer to Supervillain Stink-Man. He makes a huge jump.

He passes a plane flying next to him. Passengers wave at him. "Look! Here comes Joey the Supersocks hero!" some people say.

Supervillain Stink-man has a finger on the big red button that will send a message to the robots to release the stinking juice.

"Gotcha!" screams Joey behind him.

Supervillain Stink-Man jumps out of his chair from the shock, which gives Joey the chance to switch off the machine just in time. The robots stop moving. What an adventure that was again!

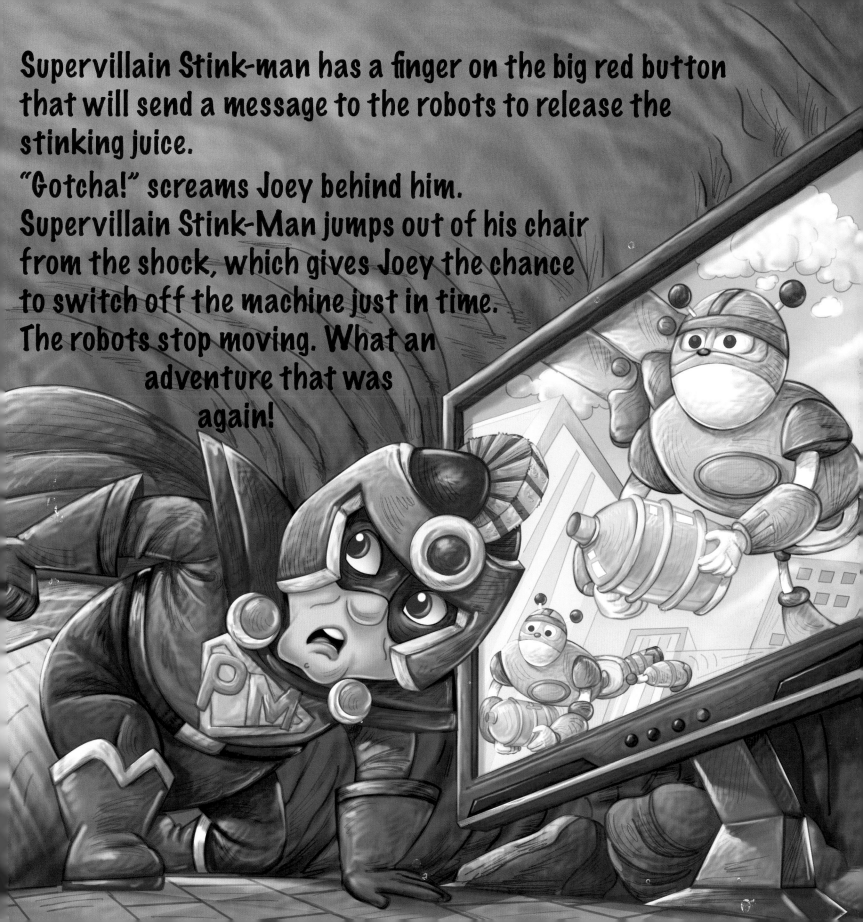

The alarm clock goes off. Joey jumps upright in his bed. Was that a dream? He would rather go right back to sleep to continue his adventures but he needs to go to school.

His socks are hanging on the back of his chair. Joey gets them. "Eww! Those socks stink!

Time to wash them!

He threw them together with the rest of the dirty clothes into the washing machine, but not before realizing that thanks to the reading and the imagination that this provokes, he himself had become a funny superhero!